For Gemk,

Whose endless supply of ideas and honest critique made this possible.

感謝 Gemk

源源不絕的靈感及誠懇的建議讓這一切成真。

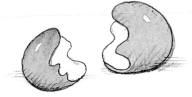

The Elephant and the Runaway Egg

大象與會跑的蛋

Coleen Reddy 著

徐鐵牛 繪

薛慧儀 譯

三民書局

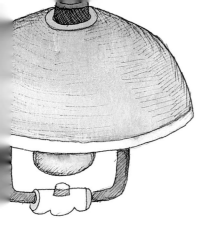

Ernie the elephant loves to eat eggs.
He eats eggs every day for breakfast.
He can cook eggs very well.

大象恩尼愛吃蛋。
他每天早餐都吃蛋。
他可以把蛋煮得很好吃喔！

4

In the morning, Ernie cooks eggs for breakfast.
He is happy. He sings as he cooks.
He cracks eggshells open with his big trunk.
Then he cooks the egg in a pan.

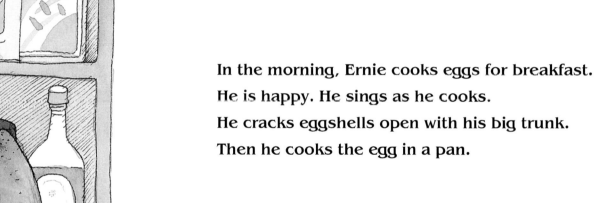

有天早上，恩尼煎蛋當早餐吃。
他好快樂，還一邊唱著歌呢！
他用大鼻子把蛋殼打破，
然後在鍋子裡煎著蛋。

He cracks the last egg open and waits for it to fall in the pan.
But he sees nothing. He looks at the eggshell and it is empty.
There is NO egg in the eggshell!

他打破最後一顆蛋的蛋殼，等著蛋掉到鍋子裡。
但是他什麼都沒看到。他看看蛋殼，裡頭居然是空的！
蛋殼裡居然沒有蛋！

"What can this mean?" says Ernie the elephant.
WHERE is the egg? Ernie is surprised.
He wants his egg.

「這是怎麼一回事？」恩尼說。
恩尼好驚訝，蛋到哪兒去了呢？
他想要他的蛋。

Ernie goes to the egg shop. He speaks to the shopkeeper.
"I want another egg," says Ernie the elephant. "The egg that
you sold to me was empty. There was nothing inside the eggshell."

恩尼來到賣蛋的店裡，跟老闆說話。
「我要另外一顆蛋，」大象恩尼說。
「你賣給我的蛋是空的，蛋殼裡什麼都沒有。」

The shopkeeper says, "That's not true.
There was an egg in the eggshell.
The egg must have run away!"

老闆說：「不對，
蛋殼裡原本有顆蛋的。
那顆蛋一定是逃走了！」

"What?" asks Ernie. "A runaway egg?"

"Yes," says the shopkeeper.

"What can I do?" asks Ernie. "I want to eat that egg."

14

「什麼?!」恩尼問。「一顆會跑的蛋?」

「沒錯。」老闆說。

「那我該怎麼辦呢?」恩尼問。「我想吃那顆蛋哪!」

"You have to look for it," says the shopkeeper. "It will not be easy."

"I will look for it," says the elephant.

So Ernie the elephant sets out to look for the runaway egg.

16

「你得去找它。」老闆說。「這可不是件容易的事喔!」
「我會去找它的。」大象說。
於是大象恩尼便出發去尋找這顆會跑的蛋了。

Ernie sees the farmer. He asks, "Did you see a runaway egg?"

"Yes, I did. It went that way," says the farmer, pointing to the woods.

"Thank you," says Ernie and he goes into the woods.

恩尼看見了農夫，他問：
「你有沒有看到一顆會跑的蛋呀？」
「有呀！它往那邊去了。」農夫一邊說，一邊指向森林。
「謝謝。」恩尼說，接著走進森林裡。

In the woods he cannot find the egg.

He asks the worm if he has seen a runaway egg.

The worm says, "No, I have not seen a runaway egg

but I can smell a runaway egg." The worm sniffs the air,

"Aha!" he says as he points to some trees, "It went that way."

他在森林裡找不到這顆蛋。
他問一隻小蟲，有沒有瞧見一顆會跑的蛋呢？
小蟲說：「沒有耶，我沒看到一顆會跑的蛋，
　但我可以嗅出一顆會跑的蛋是什麼味道。」
　　小蟲在空氣中聞了聞，「啊哈！」
他一面說一面指向幾棵大樹，「它往那邊跑了。」

Ernie goes to the tree.
He looks for the runaway egg
but he cannot find it.
Then he smells something.
It must be the egg.

恩尼走到樹邊。他東找西找，就是找不到它。
但他聞到一種味道，那一定就是這顆蛋的味道了。

There, hiding behind a tree, is the runaway egg.
"Come here, I want to eat you. You're
my egg. I bought you," says Ernie.
The egg does not move.

那顆會跑的蛋就在樹後面哪！
「過來，我要吃了你。你是我的蛋，
　我花錢買下你的。」恩尼說。
　　　但是蛋一動也不動。

The egg starts to cry.

"Don't cry, all eggs get eaten," says the elephant.

The runaway egg starts howling when the elephant says this.

蛋開始哭了起來。

「別哭嘛！蛋都是要被吃掉的啊！」大象說。

聽到恩尼這麼說，蛋就更是號啕大哭起來。

27

"What do you want?" asks Ernie.

He is tired.

It is not easy to catch a runaway egg.

「你到底想怎麼樣呢？」恩尼問。

　　他已經累了。

　　要抓住一顆會跑的蛋可真是不容易呀。

"Do you have to eat me?
Can't you eat something else?"
"Yes, I have to eat you.
What else can I do with an egg?"
asks Ernie.
"I could be your pet,"
says the runaway egg.

「你一定要吃我嗎？你不能吃別的東西嗎？」
「沒錯，我一定要吃你，
不然我要顆蛋做什麼呢？」恩尼反問。
「我可以做你的寵物呀！」會跑的蛋說。

"I don't want a pet," says Ernie. "What can I do with a pet?"

"Pets make good friends. I could talk to you," says the runaway egg.

"But where would you live?" asks the elephant. "The egg's shell is broken.

「我不想要寵物啊！」恩尼說。「我要隻寵物做什麼呢？」
「寵物可以是你的好朋友呀！我可以和你聊天喔！」會跑的蛋說。
「但你要住哪兒呢？」大象問。「蛋的殼早就打破了呀！

Fish live in bowls and birds live in cages.
Where could a pet egg live?"
"I know," says the egg. "I could live in your ear."

魚兒住在魚缸裡，鳥兒住在鳥籠裡。
一顆寵物蛋要住在哪兒呢？」
「我知道了。」蛋說。
「我可以住在你的耳朵裡呀！」

So the runaway egg becomes the elephant's pet and lives in the elephant's great, big ear. People think it looks very strange. The shopkeeper shakes his head and says, "What if the elephant gets hungry? Will he eat his pet?" But the shopkeeper doesn't know that the elephant doesn't eat eggs anymore. He says they are too gabby!

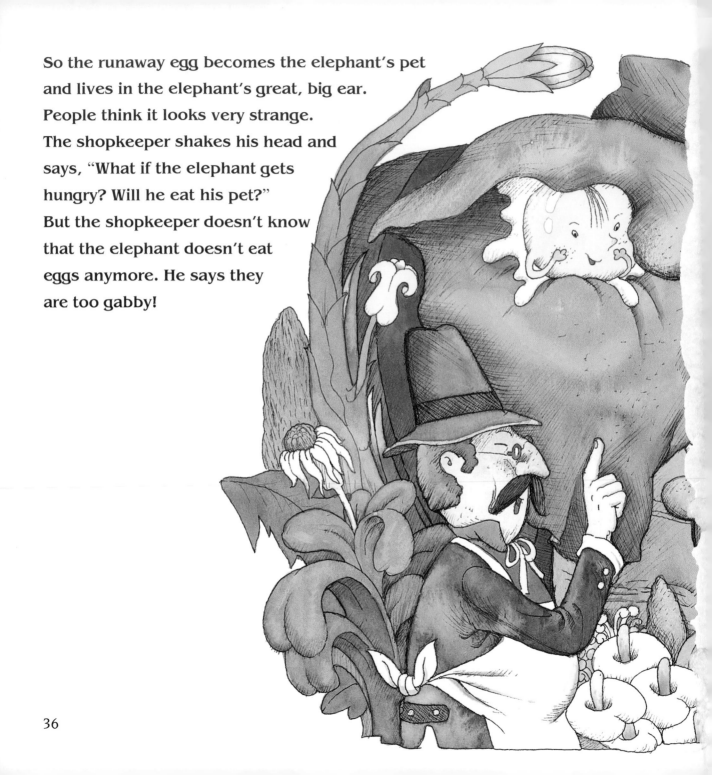

於是這顆會跑的蛋變成了大象
恩尼的寵物，而且還住在他大
大的耳朵裡頭。大家都覺得他們
這個樣子看起來真是奇怪。
賣蛋的老闆搖搖頭說：
「如果恩尼肚子餓了怎麼辦？
他會吃了自己的寵物嗎？」
但老闆不知道大象恩尼已經不再吃蛋了。
他說蛋實在是太囉唆了！

37

一起來做 夏威夷 蛋娃娃

1. 空的蛋（請媽媽或爸爸幫你把蛋白和蛋黃從蛋的底部弄出來）
2. 雙面膠
3. 棉花棒
4. 色紙
5. 塑膠瓶蓋
6. 毛線或布
7. 麥克筆
8. 剪刀

＊在做勞作之前，要記得在桌上先鋪一張紙或墊板，才不會把桌面弄得髒兮兮喔！

步驟

(1) 將蛋先用膠帶固定在塑膠瓶蓋上，再開始裝飾你的蛋娃娃，如左圖。

(2) 短褲或裙子

1. 用色紙剪一個長條形做短褲，長度與蛋的腰圍相等。

2. 將做好的短褲用雙面膠黏在蛋的腰上。

3. 黏好後，在蛋的正面與背面各剪一個小三角形，做為兩條褲管（如果是裙子就不用剪），如右圖。

(3) 衣服

1. 用色紙剪一個長條形做衣服，長度與蛋的胸圍相等。

2. 可以用色紙在衣服上加領子做裝飾。

3. 衣袖及手的部分：將棉花棒剪成二半，再用色紙剪兩個長條形，圍著棉花棒作衣袖（露出棉花棒的棉花當作手）。

4. 將衣袖用雙面膠固定在蛋的兩側。

(4) 頭部

1. 用毛線或布剪你喜歡的髮型。

2. 用雙面膠固定在蛋的頭上。

3. 最後再畫上你想要的表情就完成囉！

可以依喜好設計不一樣的造型喔！

生字表

全新創作 英文讀本
帶給你優格（yogurt）般・青春的酸甜滋味！

Teens' Chronicles

愛閱雙語叢書

青春記事簿

大維的驚奇派對／秀寶貝，說故事／杰生的大秘密
傑克的戀愛初體驗／誰是他爸爸？
叛逆大維打工記／外星老師來上課／耶！放假了！

附中英雙語CD
（共八冊）
適讀年齡：10歲以上

你我身上純真的影子，
透過一篇篇幽默風趣的故事重現，
推薦你這套青春無悔的創作系列，
讓愛玫、杰生、大維、凱爾、海倫、傑克，
帶你進入他們的世界，品味另一種學習英語的全新感受。

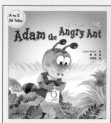

A to Z
26 Tales

二十六個妙朋友，陪你一起

愛閱雙語叢書

✿ 26個妙朋友系列 ✿

二十六個英文字母，二十六冊有趣的讀本，最適合初學英文的你！

快樂學英文！

精心錄製的雙語CD，
　　讓孩子學會正確的英文發音
用心構思的故事情節，
　　讓兒童熟悉生活中常見的單字
特別設計的親子活動，
　　讓家長和小朋友一起動動手、動動腦

中高級・中英對照 探索英文叢書

波波 唸翻天系列

你知道可愛的小兔子也會 "碎碎唸" 嗎？
波波就是這樣。
他將要告訴我們什麼有趣的故事呢？

波波的復活節／波波的西部冒險記／波波上課記／我愛你，波波
波波的下雪天／波波郊遊去／波波打球記／聖誕快樂，波波／波波的萬聖夜

共 9 本，每本均附 CD

國家圖書館出版品預行編目資料

The Elephant and the Runaway Egg:大象與會跑的
蛋 / Coleen Reddy著;徐鐵牛繪;薛慧儀譯.－－
初版一刷.－－臺北市;三民,2003
　　面;　公分－－(愛閱雙語叢書.二十六個妙朋
友系列) 中英對照
ISBN 957–14–3774–3　　(精裝)

1.英國語言－讀本

523.38　　　　　　　　　　　　　92008840

© 　The Elephant and the Runaway Egg
　　　　　　——大象與會跑的蛋

著作人	Coleen Reddy
繪　圖	徐鐵牛
譯　者	薛慧儀
發行人	劉振強
著作財產權人	三民書局股份有限公司 臺北市復興北路386號
發行所	三民書局股份有限公司 地址／臺北市復興北路386號 電話／(02)25006600 郵撥／0009998–5
印刷所	三民書局股份有限公司
門市部	復北店／臺北市復興北路386號 重南店／臺北市重慶南路一段61號

初版一刷　2003年7月
編　號　S 85638–1
定　價　新臺幣壹佰捌拾元整
行政院新聞局登記證局版臺業字第○二○○號

有著作權 · 不准侵害

ISBN　957-14-3774-3　　(精裝)

The Grumpy Goblin
壞脾氣的小妖精

Coleen Reddy 著

鄭凱軍、羅小紅 繪

薛慧儀 譯

三民書局

A gaggle of geese were playing a game of golf one day,
when the golf ball broke the window of a nearby house.
"Oh no!" said the geese. "That's the home of Gareth, the grumpy goblin."

有一天，一群鵝正在打高爾夫球。
結果一顆高爾夫球打破了附近一棟房子的窗戶。
「喔喔！糟了！」這群鵝說。「那是暴躁小妖精蓋瑞斯的家呀！」

3

A few seconds later, an angry, green goblin came storming out of his house. "How dare you break my window? What? Playing golf? That's a stupid game for geeks!" yelled Gareth the grumpy goblin.

幾秒鐘後，一隻生氣的綠色小妖精衝出屋外。
「你們居然敢打破我的窗戶！什麼？打高爾夫球？
那是怪胎才會玩的笨遊戲！」暴躁的小妖精蓋瑞斯吼著。

He was so grumpy! He grumbled so much!
The geese ran away.
All the other animals covered their ears.
The grumpy goblin made an awful noise.

他的脾氣真是太暴躁了，一直抱怨個不停！
那群鵝早就逃走了，其他動物們也都把耳朵摀了起來，
因為這個暴躁的小妖精實在太吵了！

"That's it! I've had enough of you. You're such a grumpy goblin, Gareth. Why don't you shut up?" yelled a voice.

It was a glowworm. The glowworm was glowing because it was angry.

8

「你有完沒完呀？我受夠你了！蓋瑞斯，
你真的是一個脾氣暴躁的小妖精耶！你閉嘴行不行？」有個聲音喊著。
說話的是一隻螢火蟲，因為生氣的緣故，牠正一閃一閃地發著光呢！

9

"I'm a goblin," said Gareth. "I'm supposed to be grumpy."
"That's not true," said the glowworm. "Look at me! I'm a glowworm.
Glowworms are only supposed to glow at night but I glow during the day.
I do whatever I want to."

「我是隻妖精，」蓋瑞斯說，「本來就應該要脾氣暴躁的嘛！」
「哪有這回事！」螢火蟲說。「看看我！我是隻螢火蟲，
螢火蟲應該只在晚上發光，可是我在白天也發光啊！
我想做什麼就做什麼。」

"You glow during the day because you're so stupid that you can't remember when to glow," yelled the grumpy goblin.
"You're so mean. Tell me, Gareth, why are you so mean and grumpy?"

「你在白天發光，是因為你笨到根本記不得
什麼時候該發光！」暴躁的小妖精大吼著。
「你真的很壞耶！告訴我，蓋瑞斯，你為什麼這麼壞，
脾氣又這麼暴躁呀？」

"Why should I be happy?" asked Gareth the goblin.

"Why shouldn't you be happy?" asked the glowworm.

Then to the glowworm's surprise, the goblin started crying.

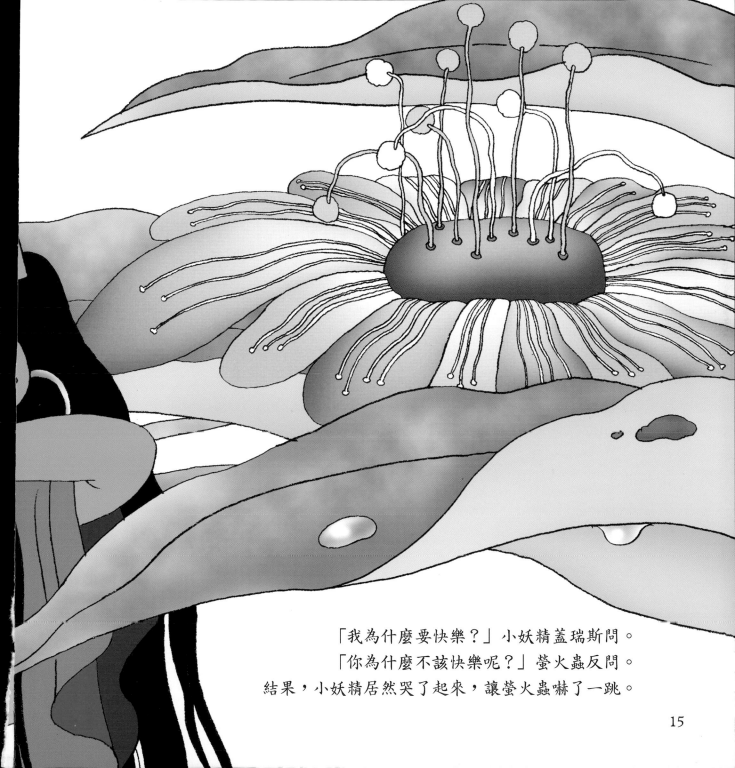

「我為什麼要快樂？」小妖精蓋瑞斯問。
「你為什麼不該快樂呢？」螢火蟲反問。
結果，小妖精居然哭了起來，讓螢火蟲嚇了一跳。

"What is it, goblin? Let it all out. It's good to cry," said the glowworm.
"It's just that...it's just that I don't like being a goblin," cried Gareth.
"Goblins are meant to be naughty and grumpy and I don't care about that.
I wanted to do something different with my life. I had dreams, you know."

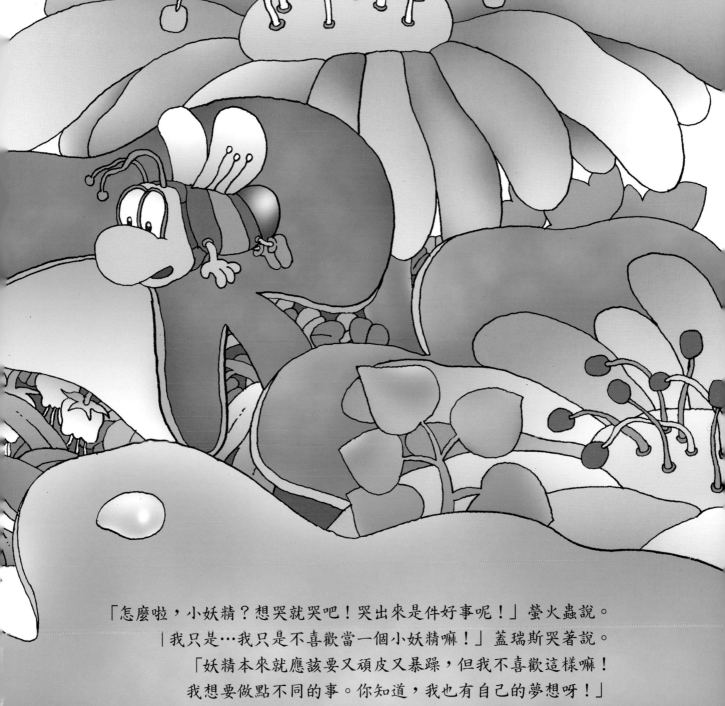

「怎麼啦，小妖精？想哭就哭吧！哭出來是件好事呢！」螢火蟲說。
「我只是…我只是不喜歡當一個小妖精嘛！」蓋瑞斯哭著說。
「妖精本來就應該要又頑皮又暴躁，但我不喜歡這樣嘛！
我想要做點不同的事。你知道，我也有自己的夢想呀！」

17

"What were your dreams?" asked the glowworm.

"It's never too late to follow your dreams."

"You'll laugh at me if I told you," said Gareth the goblin.

"No, I won't. Come on, you can tell me," said the glowworm.

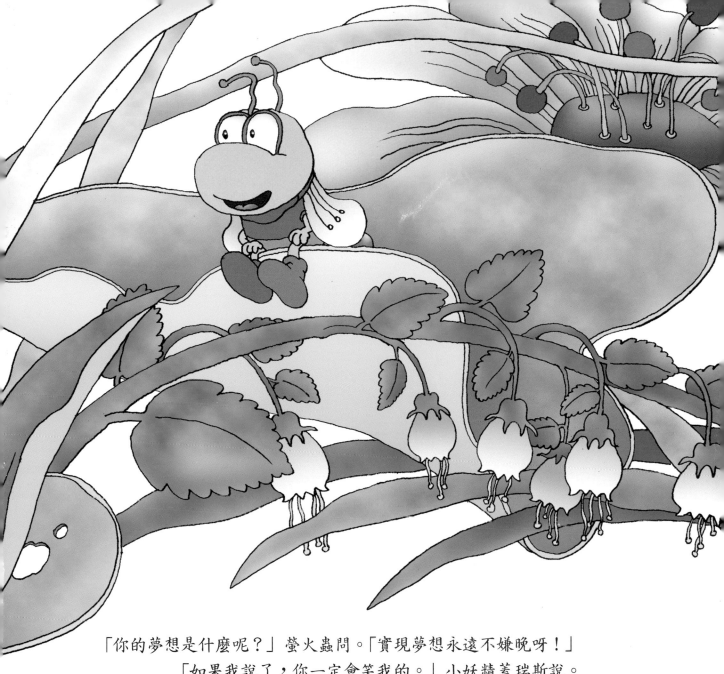

「你的夢想是什麼呢？」螢火蟲問。「實現夢想永遠不嫌晚呀！」
「如果我說了，你一定會笑我的。」小妖精蓋瑞斯說。
「我才不會呢！快點嘛！快告訴我。」螢火蟲說。

"One day, when I was a little goblin, I found a guitar in the woods.
At first I didn't know what it was but then I realized that it made music.
I taught myself how to play the guitar. I loved to play it. But when
my father found out he said that it was stupid for goblins to play the guitar.
He ordered me to stop playing the guitar."

「當我還是小小妖精的時候,有一天,我在樹林裡發現一把吉他。
剛開始我不知道那是什麼東西,後來,我發現它可以發出音樂聲,
於是我就自己學著彈吉他。我好喜歡彈吉他喔!但我爸爸發現後,
他說妖精彈吉他很愚蠢,就不准我再彈了。」

"So all my dreams of being a famous guitar player are gone,"
continued Gareth in a sad voice.
"I didn't even know you could play the guitar," said the glowworm.
"Well, I can play the guitar. Mostly, I like to play the blues."

「所以,我想成為一個吉他明星的夢想就破滅了。」
蓋瑞斯難過地繼續說著。
「我都不知道你會彈吉他呢!」螢火蟲說。
「我當然會囉!而且大部分的時候我喜歡彈奏藍調。」

"Why don't you play some blues for us now?" said the glowworm.

"No, I told you. Goblins aren't supposed to play the guitar."

"I, for one, don't believe that you even know what a guitar looks like. You're just lying. All goblins are the same. You can't believe anything they say," said a bird that had been listening to their conversation.

The goblin was furious. "I'll show you!"

He went into his house to get his guitar.

「何不現在就為我們彈些藍調呢？」螢火蟲說。

「不行，我告訴過你了，小妖精是不應該彈吉他的。」

「我啊，甚至不相信你知道吉他長什麼樣子呢！你根本就是在說謊。

所有的小妖精都一樣！千萬不要相信他們說的話。」

一隻剛剛聽到他們對話的小鳥說著。

小妖精氣壞了。「我證明給你看！」他馬上走進屋子去拿吉他。

When he came outside, there were lots of animals
waiting to hear him play the blues.
Gareth began to play and sing.
He sang a sad song and all the animals thought it was touching.
The glowworm started crying and soon everyone was crying.
When Gareth finished, all the animals started clapping.

他走出來的時候，外頭已經圍了好多動物，
等著聽他彈奏藍調。蓋瑞斯開始彈吉他並唱起歌來。
他唱了一首感傷的歌，所有的動物都覺得這首歌好感人哪！
螢火蟲哭了起來，很快地，大家全都哭成一片。
蓋瑞斯演唱完畢時，所有的動物都鼓掌叫好。

Gareth the goblin is now a famous guitar player.
He plays at weddings and at birthday parties.
He isn't grumpy anymore.

小妖精蓋瑞斯
現在是一個出名的　　　吉他手了！他在婚禮或是
生日宴會上演奏吉他。他的脾氣再也不暴躁了喔！

The goblin's story has inspired other animals.

The geese have started playing professional golf.

The glowworm...? Well, the glowworm decided to go to Hollywood.

His dream is to be a prop in a movie.

We'll have to see it to believe it.

小妖精的故事也啟發了其他動物唷！
那群鵝開始進軍職業高爾夫球賽了。
而螢火蟲呢？嗯，螢火蟲決定到好萊塢去。他的夢想是成為
電影裡的小道具。結果如何呢？那要等我們親眼看見才知道囉！

31

聽寫拼字遊戲
Crosswords

小朋友，讓我們跟著小妖精和螢火蟲一起來玩這個遊戲，玩之前先按下 track 3，跟著小妖精和螢火蟲把單字念兩遍，然後按下 track 4 之後，你會聽到中文題目的部分，但括弧裡的中文會用英文念出來，這個時候呢，你就要把英文拼出來，跟著題號填在表中。

dream   grumpy   guitar   wedding

clap   prop   blues   naughty

mean   golf   glowworm   goblin

直的 (Down)

1. ![bug]問![creature]說：「你為什麼這麼（壞）」？

2. ![creature]最喜歡彈奏（藍調）。

3. 那群![creatures]很怕![creature]，因為他的脾氣非常地（暴躁）。

4. ![creature]在（婚禮）上演奏音樂。

5. ![bug]決定到好萊塢去當電影裡的（小道具）。

6. （吉他）是![creature]最拿手的樂器。

7. 那群![creatures]在打（高爾夫球）的時候，打破了一扇窗戶。

橫的 (Across)

(1) ![creature]的（夢想）是成為一個吉他明星。

(2) ![creature]的爸爸說，（妖精）彈吉他是很愚蠢的。

(3) ![bug]告訴![creature]說（螢火蟲）只在晚上發光。

(4) ![creature]表演完之後，所有的動物都（鼓掌）叫好。

(5) 妖精應該要（頑皮）又暴躁。

生字表

 p. 2

gaggle [`gægḷ] 名 鵝群

grumpy [`grʌmpɪ] 形 脾氣壞的

goblin [`gablɪn] 名 小妖精

 p. 4

storm out 猛衝

geek [gik] 名 怪人

 p. 6

grumble [`grʌmbḷ] 動 抱怨

awful [`ɔfʊl] 形 可怕的，嚇人的

 p. 8

yell [jɛl] 動 大聲喊叫

glowworm [`glo,wɝm] 名 螢火蟲

glow [glo] 動 發光

 p. 10

be supposed to 應該

 p. 12

mean [min] 形 惡劣的

p. 22

blues [bluz] 形 藍調

p. 24

furious [`fjʊrɪəs] 形 狂怒的

p. 26

touching [`tʌtʃɪŋ] 形 感人的

p. 30

professional [prə`fɛʃənḷ] 形 職業的

prop [prɑp] 名 小道具

解答

全新創作 英文讀本
帶給你優格（yogurt）般．青春的酸甜滋味！

Teens' Chronicles

愛閱雙語叢書

青春記事簿

大維的驚奇派對／秀寶貝，說故事／杰生的大秘密
傑克的戀愛初體驗／誰是他爸爸？
叛逆大維打工記／外星老師來上課／耶！放假了！

你我身上純真的影子，
透過一篇篇幽默風趣的故事重現，
推薦你這套青春無悔的創作系列，
讓愛玫、杰生、大維、凱爾、海倫、傑克，
帶你進入他們的世界，品味另一種學習英語的全新感受。

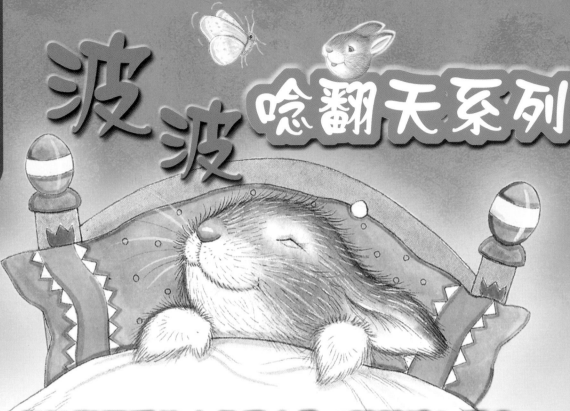

國家圖書館出版品預行編目資料

The Grumpy Goblin:壞脾氣的小妖精／Coleen Reddy著；鄭凱軍，羅小紅繪；薛慧儀譯.－－初版一刷.－－臺北市；三民，2003
　　　面；　公分－－(愛閱雙語叢書.二十六個妙朋友系列) 中英對照
ISBN 957－14－3772－7　（精裝）

1.英國語言－讀本

523.38　　　　　　　　　　　　92008838

© **The Grumpy Goblin**
——壞脾氣的小妖精

著作人　Coleen Reddy
繪　圖　鄭凱軍　羅小紅
譯　者　薛慧儀
發行人　劉振強
著作財
產權人　三民書局股份有限公司
　　　　臺北市復興北路386號
發行所　三民書局股份有限公司
　　　　地址／臺北市復興北路386號
　　　　電話／(02)25006600
　　　　郵撥／0009998－5
印刷所　三民書局股份有限公司
門市部　復北店／臺北市復興北路386號
　　　　重南店／臺北市重慶南路一段61號
初版一刷　2003年7月
　編　號　S 85640－1
　定　價　新臺幣壹佰捌拾元整
行政院新聞局登記證局版臺業字第○二○○號

ISBN　957－14－3772－7　　（精裝）